break all rules

By Eleanor Robins

SADDLEBACK
EDUCATIONAL PUBLISHING

SADDLEBACK
EDUCATIONAL PUBLISHING
www.sdlback.com

ISBN-13: 978-1-61651-590-4
ISBN-10: 1-61651-590-2
eBook: 978-1-61247-236-2

Printed in Malaysia

21 20 19 18 17   6 7 8 9 10

Meet the Characters from

break all rules

Anna: dates Cole

Coach Brent: coaches the Dawson High football team

Cole: dates Anna, plays tight end for the Dawson High football team, is Jeff's best friend

Garrett: plays running back for the Oak Hill High football team, is their best player

Jeff: plays tight end for the Dawson High football team, is Cole's best friend

Rick: plays back-up center for the Dawson High football team, breaks rules

chapter 1

It was Friday night. Cole was at home. He had his radio on. His cell phone chirped. He had a text message from Anna. Anna was his girlfriend. Anna texted, "Call me."

Cole turned the radio down. Then he called Anna. "Hi, Anna. When did you get home?" Cole asked. Anna had gone to see her little sister Sara's play. That was why she and Cole didn't have a date.

"A few minutes ago," Anna said.

"How was the play? Did you have a

good time?" Cole asked.

Anna said, "The play was okay. But I wish you'd been there with me. Where are you now? What have you been doing tonight?"

Cole said, "I'm at home. I have the radio on. I'm trying to find out the Oak Hill game's score."

The winner of the game would play Dawson High in the state finals. Cole was on the Dawson High team. He played tight end.

He hoped that Oak Hill lost. Oak Hill had the best team in the state. And Cole didn't want to play them in the state finals.

Oak Hill had the best running back in the state. His name was Garrett. And Cole didn't think Oak Hill could lose with him on the team.

Anna said, "I'll hang up. You can listen to the radio."

"You don't have to hang up. I can find out the score later. I'm sure Oak Hill will win," Cole said.

"I'll still hang up. I know you want to find out the score right away. You can call me tomorrow morning," Anna said.

"Okay. I'll talk to you then," Cole said.

Cole turned the radio back up. He thought about the Oak Hill game. Cole couldn't keep his mind on his homework.

About twenty minutes later, his cell phone rang. He turned the radio down. Then he quickly answered his phone.

A boy said, "Bro, it's Jeff. I just found out who won the Oak Hill game."

Jeff was Cole's best friend. Jeff was on the Dawson High team. And he was a tight end, too.

"Great. Who won?" Cole asked.

"Bad news. Oak Hill won," Jeff said. "I just heard it on the radio. Oak Hill won by 21 points."

"That doesn't surprise me. But I hoped they would lose," Cole said.

Jeff said, "Yeah, me too. That Garrett guy's a good player. I don't think we can beat Oak Hill in the state finals."

"We need to believe we can win. If we don't, we won't have a chance," said Cole

"Yeah. I know. I'll try to think we can win. But I don't believe we can. Unless something happens," Jeff said.

"Like what?" Cole asked.

"I don't know. But maybe something will happen that will help us. We need all the help we can get," Jeff said.

"You're right about that," Cole said.

The only thing that would help was if Garrett didn't play. And Cole didn't want Garrett to get hurt. Cole couldn't think of anything else that could help Dawson High win.

chapter 2

It was Monday afternoon. Cole was at football practice. Jeff was there, too. They were talking about the Oak Hill game. Their friend Rick ran over to them. Rick was the back-up center.

Rick said, "I don't know why I came to football practice today."

"What do you mean by that?" Cole asked.

Jeff said, "Yeah. What do you mean by that? We all have to practice. So we have to be here today."

"There isn't any reason to practice. We'll still lose on Saturday. There's no way we can beat Oak Hill. So why practice?" Rick asked.

Coach Brent blew his whistle. He was the football coach.

Coach Brent yelled to the team. He said, "Guys, all of you come over here. We need to get started." The boys ran over to him.

Coach Brent said, "I think all of you already know this. We'll play Oak Hill in Macon on Saturday afternoon."

Cole knew the coach was right. All of the players knew it. And none of them were happy about it. They didn't want to play Oak Hill. Their winning streak would be over.

Coach Brent said, "I want you to be rested for the game. So we'll go to Macon after school on Friday."

"That sounds good to me," Jeff said.

Cole was glad about that, too. He wouldn't have to get up early on Saturday. And then ride on a bus to Macon most of the morning.

Coach Brent said, "Our game with Oak Hill will be a tough one. And you will need to work hard all week. You will need to be at your best for the game."

"Why does it matter, Coach?" Rick asked.

Cole couldn't believe Rick asked the coach that. Some of the other players looked surprised, too.

Coach Brent looked at Rick. He didn't look pleased with Rick. "What do you mean by that, Rick?" he asked.

Rick said, "We have to play Oak Hill. And Oak Hill is the best team in the state. There's no way we can beat them. Not with that dude Garrett on the team."

"That's the wrong way to think, Rick," Coach Brent said.

"Yeah, Rick," Cole said.

"Yeah," some of the other boys said.

"You're wrong, Rick. We'll beat them," said another boy.

"Yeah," most of the boys said. But not all of them looked as though they believed it.

Rick said, "No way. We'll never be able to beat Oak Hill."

Coach Brent looked at Rick again. He still didn't look pleased.

He said, "You might be right, Rick. But you need to think about something."

"What?" Rick asked.

Coach Brent said, "On any day the best team can lose. And on any day the team that isn't the best team can win."

Cole knew that was true.

Coach Brent said, "We might not be as good as Oak Hill. But this Saturday could be their day to lose. So we have to be ready to win."

Coach Brent told the team about some other teams that had won. No one had thought they had a chance to win. But they won anyway.

Then Coach Brent said, "So think about that, Rick. And all of you guys think about that, too. We might be able to beat Oak Hill. But you have to practice hard. You must be ready to beat them."

Coach Brent looked at all of the boys. Then he looked back at Rick.

"Anything else you'd like to say, Rick?" he asked.

"No," Rick said.

Then Rick looked down at the ground.

Cole said, "Coach Brent is right. We need to practice hard. Then we'll be ready to beat Oak Hill on Saturday."

Cole still wasn't sure they could beat Oak Hill.

chapter 3

It was Friday afternoon. Cole sat on the school bus. He was sitting with Jeff. They were on their way to Macon.

Coach Brent was on the bus, too. And some of the football team was on the bus. The rest of the players were on two other school buses.

Jeff said, "I sure am glad we're going to Macon today—not tomorrow morning."

Cole said, "Me, too. That means we can sleep later tomorrow. And we won't be tired from riding the bus all morning."

"Yeah. We need all the rest we can get," Jeff said.

Coach Brent got up from his seat behind the driver. He yelled back to the team.

"Guys, we'll get off at the next exit," said the coach. "Then we'll stop and get something to eat."

Coach Brent sat down in the seat behind the bus driver.

The driver pulled onto the exit ramp. He stopped at the top of the exit ramp. He turned right. He drove about a mile. Then he pulled into a parking lot next to a restaurant. And he parked the bus.

Jeff said, "I don't believe it. Look who's here."

"Yeah. I see them," Cole said.

Three Oak Hill buses were in the parking lot. The Oak Hill football players were walking to the buses.

Coach Brent stood up again. He yelled back to the Dawson High team. "Be nice, guys. Don't make any trouble with the Oak Hill team."

Then Coach Brent got off of the bus. He stood at the door of the bus. And he watched the Dawson High team get off of the bus.

Some of the Oak Hill boys were playing with a football. One of them yelled over to the Dawson team.

"We'll win! And we'll be number one!" he yelled.

Cole and Jeff and some of the other Dawson High boys yelled back.

"You're wrong. We'll win. And we'll be number one," they yelled.

The Oak Hill players got on their buses. Then the buses pulled out of the parking lot.

The Dawson High team started to

walk toward the restaurant.

Jeff said, "I sure wish we could beat Oak Hill. But I don't think we can."

Cole said, "We have to believe we can win. If we don't, we won't have a chance."

"Yeah. You said that before, bro. Something will have to happen to help us. Or Oak Hill will win," Jeff said.

Cole knew that it was true. But he didn't know what that something might be.

chapter 4

It was two hours later. Cole and Jeff sat on the bus. Coach Brent and some of the football team were on the bus, too. They were on their way to the motel where the team would stay.

Jeff said, "I hope we're almost there. I'm tired of sitting on the bus."

"I'm ready to get there, too," Cole said.

The boys rode for about ten more minutes. And they talked about the game. Then the bus driver pulled into a motel parking lot.

Jeff said, "Oh, no. The Oak Hill buses are here. The Oak Hill players must be staying here, too."

"How did that happen?" Cole asked. He knew Jeff didn't know the answer to that.

"I can't believe they are staying here," Jeff said.

The bus driver drove through the parking lot for a few yards. Then he parked the bus.

Coach Brent got up from his seat behind the driver. He yelled back to the team.

"I don't know how this could happen, guys. But the Oak Hill players are staying here, too," said Coach Brent. "Try to stay away from them as much as you can. And don't make any trouble with them."

Cole hoped the Oak Hill players would stay away from the Dawson High team. And he hoped they wouldn't make any trouble.

Coach Brent said, "I need to tell the motel staff we're here. All of you stay on the bus."

"Okay, Coach," some of the boys yelled back to him. Coach Brent got off the bus. And he went inside the motel.

Three Oak Hill players came out of the front door of the motel. They stopped when they saw the Dawson High buses.

Then the three boys walked over to Cole's bus. They yelled through the windows to the Dawson High team.

"We'll beat you tomorrow. You can count on it," one of the boys said.

"Yeah. You can count on it," a second boy said.

The first one said, "We have Garrett. He's the best running back in the state."

The third boy said, "That's me. I'm

Garrett. We'll beat you tomorrow. By three or four touchdowns. You can count on it."

"Yeah, Garrett. By three or four touchdowns," the first boy said.

Rick yelled out the window to them. "Get lost," he yelled.

Some of the Dawson High players got up from their seats. Cole was worried they might get off the bus. They might even go after the Oak Hill players.

Two Oak Hill coaches ran up to the bus. One of them yelled, "Get back to your rooms, guys. Stay away from the Dawson High team."

Garrett looked at the boys on the bus. He said, "See you tomorrow, guys." Then he laughed.

Garrett started to walk back to the motel. The other two Oak Hill players followed him.

One Oak Hill coach looked at the Dawson High players. He said, "Sorry about that, guys. It won't happen again."

Rick put his head out of the bus window. He yelled, "It better not. Or your players will be sorry."

The two coaches walked away.
Rick put his head back inside the bus. He said, "I wish we could beat that team."

"I wish we could, too," Cole said.

Oak Hill was too good. Cole didn't think there was any way Dawson High could beat them. Not with Garrett on the team.

chapter 5

It was later that night. Cole and Jeff were in their motel room. Rick was there, too.

Rick said, "I think I'll go to the vending machines. They're in that room down the hall. I'll buy something to eat."

"I don't think you should do that. You might see some of the Oak Hill players. Coach Brent told us to stay away from them," Cole said.

"I'm not afraid of the Oak Hill players. I'll be back in a few minutes," Rick said.

Rick opened the door. He hurried outside. Then he closed the door.

Jeff asked, "Do you think we should go with him?"

"Maybe. But we might see some of the Oak Hill players. I don't want to get into any trouble with them. If we did, the coach wouldn't let us play tomorrow," Cole said.

"Yeah. You're right about that," Jeff said.

Jeff turned on the TV. Cole and Jeff started to watch a show. They liked the show. So they didn't think about how long Rick had been gone.

Soon the show ended. But Rick hadn't come back to their room.

Cole looked at his watch. He said, "Oh, no."

"What?" Jeff asked.

"Rick has been gone more than 30

minutes. He should have been back by now. Something must have happened to him," Cole said.

Cole was worried about Rick. Jeff looked worried about Rick, too.

Jeff asked, "What do you think happened to him? Do you think he saw some of the Oak Hill players? Maybe he got into trouble with them."

"I hope not. But I'm worried that he might have," Cole said.

"Do you think we should tell Coach Brent that he went to the vending machines? And that he hasn't come back?" Jeff asked.

Cole said, "No. Maybe Rick is okay. I don't want to worry the coach about nothing. So let's wait. Maybe Rick will come back in a few minutes."

The boys tried to watch some more TV. They couldn't keep their minds on the show. Ten more minutes went by.

Cole said, "I think we should go and look for Rick."

"I think we should, too. Where should we go first?" Jeff asked.

"To the vending machines. Maybe Rick's still there. Maybe he's talking to one of our players," Cole said.

"Let's go," Jeff said. The two boys walked to the door. Cole opened the door. They quickly went outside.

Jeff asked, "Do you have our room key?"

Cole made sure he had the room key. "Yeah. I have it," he said. Then he closed the door.

The two boys hurried to the vending machines. Cole hoped they would see Rick along the way. But they didn't. They didn't see any Oak Hill players either. Cole was glad about that.

Cole and Jeff got to the room with the vending machines. The door was closed. Someone was beating on the inside of the door.

Then Cole heard Rick's voice from inside the room. "Let me out. Let me out. I can't get out of here!" he yelled.

Jeff asked, "Rick, is that you? Are you in there?"

"Yeah. Let me out. I can't get the door open. It's stuck," Rick said.

Cole said, "Dude, move back from the door. I'll try to open it."

"Okay," Rick said.

Cole pushed on the door. He got it open. Rick hurried out of the room.

"Thanks. I could have been in there all night," Rick said.

Cole was glad they found Rick. He was relieved that an Oak Hill player didn't find Rick.

Rick said, "I sure am glad this happened tonight. Not tomorrow before the game. I could have been in there for hours. And I might have missed the bus to the game."

"Yeah. Then you couldn't have played," Jeff said.

Cole didn't want any of the Dawson High players to miss the game. Dawson High mightn't be able to win. But all of the players needed to be there so the team would have a chance.

Cole knew what he should do tomorrow. He must check the vending machines before they left for the game. He would make sure a Dawson High player wasn't trapped in there.

chapter 6

It was the next morning. Cole was on his way to breakfast. Jeff and Rick were with him.

A door opened. Garrett came out of a room. He almost bumped into the three boys.

Garrett said, "Well, well, well. Look who's here. Some of the Dawson High losers."

Cole didn't like what Garrett said. But he didn't say anything. Cole wanted to play in the game. So he didn't want to get into any trouble.

Rick said, "We haven't lost yet." Rick looked mad. And he sounded mad.

"Oh you will. Just wait and see," Garrett said. Then Garrett laughed. He started to walk away.

Rick yelled after him, "You'll be sorry that you called us losers."

Garrett stopped. He turned around. Then he looked at Rick. Garrett said, "I won't be sorry. But you'll be sorry that you played my team in the state finals. We'll beat you by three or four touchdowns."

Garrett started to walk away again. Rick went to go after him. Cole said, "Don't. It isn't worth it. You don't want to get into any trouble."

"Cole is right, Rick. Don't go after him. It's not worth it," Jeff said.

Rick stopped. He didn't say anything more. But Cole knew he was still mad.

The three boys went to breakfast. They ate quickly.

Then they went back to their room. They stayed there for a while. Then it was time for the team to go to the football stadium.

The boys left the motel room. They walked to the bus.

Rick said, "I wish we could beat Oak Hill. We could show Garrett that we aren't losers. I wish something would happen to Garrett. Then he can't play today."

"You shouldn't wish that," Cole said.

"I know. But that's how I feel," Rick said.

Then Cole thought of something. And he was glad that he did.

"We need to check the vending

machines," said Cole. "We need to make sure that none of our players are stuck in that room. We don't want to leave anyone behind."

Jeff said, "Our players know it's time to get on the bus. So I don't think any of them would be in there."

"I don't think they are. But I want to make sure they aren't," Cole said.

"Okay," Jeff said. The three boys walked to the vending machines.

When they got near the room, they heard someone beating on the door. A boy was yelling from inside.

"Let me out. Let me out. I have to get out of here," the boy yelled.

Then Cole heard a horn blow.

Jeff said, "That sounds like one of our buses. We need to get to our bus."

"Yeah. We do," Cole said.

Rick said, "I'll let him out. You two can

go on to the bus. I'll be there in a minute. Don't let the bus leave without me."

"We won't. But hurry, Rick," Cole said.

"Yeah. Hurry," Jeff said.

Rick went over to the door. Cole heard the boy yell something to Rick. But Cole didn't hear what the boy said.

Rick didn't need any help. He could get the door open by himself. Cole and Jeff hurried to the bus.

chapter
7

Cole stood on the sidelines with Jeff. It was almost time for the game to start. Cole looked at the people in the stands.

Jeff asked, "What are you doing?"

"Looking for Anna. She said she would come to the game. I know she's here. But I don't see her," Cole said.

"You don't really think you can see her in this crowd, do you?" Jeff asked.

"No. Not really. But I have to look for her," Cole said. Cole knew he wouldn't be able to see Anna. So he looked at the Oak Hill team.

Some of the players kept going in and out of their locker room. Two of the Oak Hill coaches went in the locker room, too.

Cole looked over at Jeff. He asked, "What do you think is going on? The Oak Hill players keep going in and out of their locker room. And now two coaches just went in."

"I don't know. But they all act like they're looking for something," Jeff said.

"Yeah. They do. I wonder what," Cole said.

Rick walked over to them. "What are you guys talking about?" he asked.

"Some Oak Hill players keep going in and out of their locker room. And two of the coaches just went in. We don't know why," Cole said.

"Maybe they're looking for someone," Rick said,

"Who?" Cole asked.

"Yeah. Who?" Jeff asked.

"How would I know?" Rick asked. Rick laughed and then walked away.

"Why did Rick laugh?" Jeff asked.

"Who knows? You know how Rick is," Cole said.

Coach Erwin walked over to Coach Brent. Coach Erwin was the Oak Hill coach. He had a worried look on his face.

The Dawson High team stopped talking. They wanted to hear what the two men said to each other.

Coach Brent asked, "What's wrong, Coach Erwin? Is there a problem?"

"There sure is. I can't find one of my players," Coach Erwin said.

"You can't find one of your players?" Coach Brent asked. He sounded very surprised. And he looked very surprised, too.

"Garrett didn't get to the field. We looked in the locker room. He isn't there. We can't find him anywhere," Coach Erwin said.

Cole looked over at Jeff. Jeff looked as surprised as he was. Cole looked at Rick. Rick didn't look surprised. Rick had a smile on his face.

Coach Brent said, "It doesn't make sense. Are you sure he came to the stadium with your team?"

"I didn't see Garrett on my bus. But I thought he was on another bus. And I haven't seen him here. But two of the guys said they saw him here. So he must be here somewhere," Coach Erwin said.

Rick started to cough. And he coughed and coughed some more.

Coach Brent looked at Rick. "Are you

all right, Rick?" he asked.

"Yeah. I'm fine," Rick said.

Rick looked fine. And he still had a smile on his face.

Coach Erwin said, "I sent two coaches inside to look for Garrett. But they couldn't find him."

"I wish we could help you. But we don't know where Garrett is," Coach Brent said.

Rick started to cough again.

Coach Brent looked at Rick again. "Are you sure you're all right, Rick?" he asked.

"Yeah, Coach. I'm fine," Rick said.

Rick still looked fine. And he still had a smile on his face.

Cole didn't really know what Rick was thinking. But Cole thought he knew.

Rick thought Dawson High had a chance to win now that Oak Hill couldn't find Garrett. Oak Hill might be able to win without him. But Cole didn't think they could. He was sure that Rick thought the same thing.

Cole hoped Garrett was okay. But where was he? Would he show in time to play?

chapter 8

It was time for the game to start. Garrett was still not there. Coach Erwin walked over to Coach Brent.

The Dawson High boys stopped talking. They wanted to hear the two men talk.

Coach Erwin said, "We still can't find Garrett."

Coach Brent asked, "Are you sure he came to the stadium? Maybe he's still at the motel."

Rick said, "Maybe he didn't want to

play in the game. So he just left."

Coach Erwin said, "Garrett wouldn't do that. He would never let the team down that way."

"Are you sure you didn't leave him at the motel?" Coach Brent asked.

Coach Erwin said, "No. I'm not sure about that. But Garrett would have called by now if we had left him behind. Unless something has happened to him."

"I'm sure he's all right," Coach Brent said. But Coach Brent didn't look so sure about that.

Coach Erwin said, "We were all at the same motel. Did any of your players see anything? Do they know where Garrett might be?"

Coach Brent looked surprised that Coach Erwin had asked him that.

Coach Brent said, "My guys play fair. They don't know why your player isn't here. They would tell me if they did."

A referee walked over to the two men. He said, "Time to start the game. Get ready to play."

"We're ready. And we've been ready," Rick said.

Cole looked at Rick. Rick had a big smile on his face.

Cole got a bad feeling about Rick.

Then Cole thought of something. Now he was sure he knew where Garrett was.

Cole walked over to Rick. He said, "I need to talk to you, dude. Over there." Cole pointed to a place where no one else was standing.

The two boys walked away from the others.

Rick asked, "What do you want?"

Rick didn't have a smile on his face. Cole thought Rick knew what he wanted to ask him.

Cole said, "You know where Garrett is."

"How would I know where he is? He just didn't want to play. So he left," Rick said.

"You know that isn't true. And you know where he is," Cole said. "Garrett was stuck with the vending machines at the motel. He's the one you went to let out. But when you found out who he was, you didn't let him out," Cole said.

"You're wrong. I let him out. And he wasn't Garrett," Rick said.

But Cole knew he was right. He could tell by the look on Rick's face. Cole walked away.

"Where are you going?" Rick asked.

Cole stopped. He looked back at Rick. "To tell Coach Brent where Garrett is," Cole said.

"Don't do that, Cole. We might win if

Garrett doesn't play. You know that. It's his fault he got stuck in that room, not ours," Rick said.

"It's our fault Garrett is still in there," Cole said. He should have made sure Rick let the boy out. Cole started to walk away.

Rick said, "Don't do it. Don't tell the coach."

Cole stopped and he looked back at Rick. "Our team plays fair. At least the rest of us do."

Then Cole ran over to Coach Brent. He would tell him where to find Garrett.

Cole was sure that Oak Hill would win now with Garrett back in action. But it would be a fair game. That was how the game should be played.

consider this...

1. How far would you go to make sure your team won an important game?

2. How would you react if someone called you a loser?

3. What could the Dawson High boys have done to avoid getting into an argument with the Oak Hill team?

4. What does Rick's wish that something might happen to Garrett tell us about him?

5. Have you ever had a bad feeling about somebody or something? What was it and what did you do?